BRATZ™

Good-Luck Charms

By Holly Kowitt

SCHOLASTIC INC.

New York   Toronto   London   Auckland   Sydney
Mexico City   New Delhi   Hong Kong   Buenos Aires

ISBN-10: 0-439-91951-7
ISBN-13: 978-0-439-91951-7

Designed by Jenn Martino

12 11 10 9 8 7 6 5 4   7 8 9 10/0

Printed in the U.S.A.
First printing, February 2007

Chapter 1

"Can I have your attention, class?" asked Mr. O'Shea, the creative-writing teacher, clearing his throat.

They had just finished the journal-writing exercise that Mr. O'Shea ended every class with, and which Yasmin totally loved! Cloe and Sasha had written theirs quickly, and were now bent over one of their favorite fashion magazines checking out a spread on cute camouflage jackets. They were headed to a mountain lodge known for its spectacular views and amazing hiking trails this weekend, and they needed every spare moment to plan their trip! But now that Mr. O'Shea was calling an official end to journal-writing time, they quickly closed the magazine and turned their attention back to their teacher.

The girls all loved their creative-writing class, because Mr. O'Shea was an awesome teacher. But Yasmin planned to be a writer one day, so she was especially into this class, and immediately shushed her best friends Cloe, Jade, and Sasha whenever their teacher had something to say.

"I have a very special writing assignment for all of you," Mr. O'Shea continued. "In honor of St. Patrick's Day, I'd like each of you to write an essay about your good-luck charms."

"Good-luck charms?" asked Jade, caught by surprise.

"Yes," said Mr. O'Shea. "Choose something that you feel has brought you good luck, such as a lucky sweater or a lucky penny, and explain why you believe this item is good luck for you — like you always have a really good day when you wear it, or seem to win every game when you're carrying it."

"That's a really cool assignment, Mr. O'Shea!" Cloe exclaimed. Then she clapped her hand over her mouth, embarrassed to have interrupted him.

"So glad you approve," he said with a smile. "Does that mean you have an idea for what you might write about?"

"My camera," blurted Cloe. "It always gives me awesome shots of all my friends — it's almost like it's magic!" Sasha, Jade, and Yasmin giggled. Cloe was constantly snapping pictures, whether it was at one of their spectacular sleepovers, an amazing weekend trip, on a trip to the mall, or just in the school cafeteria. Cloe was a bit of a photo addict! But she just had so much fun with her best friends that she wanted to make sure she captured all of the memories. And since she was totally artistic, her photos always came out looking gorgeous. The girls all thought Cloe would make a fabulous fashion photographer one day.

"That sounds like a really fun essay, Cloe," said Mr. O'Shea. "I look forward to reading it. And to reading everyone else's, too!"

Sasha, always practical, shot her hand into the air, and the teacher called on her. "Mr. O'Shea, what if I don't have a lucky charm?"

Mr. O'Shea raised his eyebrows and replied, "You're a smart girl, Sasha. I'm sure you'll come up with something. But you better make it quick — these essays are due on Monday."

Monday! The girls exchanged worried glances. They'd have to get cranking on the assignment right away, because tomorrow after school, they were heading up to the mountains in Cloe's cruiser.

As they filed out of class, Cloe, Yasmin, and Jade chatted excitedly about the assignment, while Sasha trailed behind, looking anxious.

"Mr. O'Shea always comes up with the coolest writing assignments," Jade exclaimed.

"So what are you going to write about, Kool Kat?" Cloe asked. Jade was always dressed in totally cutting-edge fashions, and she was always designing amazing looks of her own. Her fabulous fashion sense had earned her the nickname "Kool Kat," and her friends knew she was going to be a famous fashion designer one day.

"My lucky zebra-print notebook, of course!" she replied, pulling it out of her bookbag. "Whenever I use it, super-cool fashion designs just seem to pour out of my head."

"That sounds so cool!" Yasmin exclaimed. "I'm going to write about my lucky new denim jacket." Yasmin had found a perfect new jacket a couple of weeks ago, and ever since, anytime she couldn't quite get a look to work, she'd throw on the jacket with anything from jeans to a dress and suddenly she looked totally cool.

"So, Sash, what're you gonna write about?" Jade asked, noticing that her friend hadn't said a word.

"I have no clue," Sasha replied. "I mean, I really don't believe in good-luck charms."

"What?" Cloe gasped. "Why not?" Cloe could be really dramatic and definitely believed in things outside of the normal world. In fact she sometimes got totally caught up in her own little dream-world, and her friends had to pull her back down to earth. Combined with her heavenly style, which seemed to let her float down the halls of Stiles

High, Cloe's tendency to have her head in the clouds had earned her the nickname "Angel."

"I just think people make their own luck," Sasha replied.

"But haven't you ever had, like, a lucky CD or dance shoes or something?" Yasmin prodded. Sasha was totally into music — she was sure to be a famous record producer one day — and her friends called her "Bunny Boo" because of her urban-cool style.

"No," Sasha replied. "I haven't. I just can't believe Mr. O'Shea would give us such a dumb assignment."

"But I think it'll be fun!" Cloe protested. "Come on, there must be something — what about your electric guitar?" When their band, the Rock Angelz, had held their huge concert in London, Sasha had totally rocked on her shiny red guitar. That girl had mad musical skills!

"Or your sky-blue handbag," suggested Jade. Sasha's stylish little purse added instant style and color to any outfit.

But Sasha just shook her head sadly. The guitar was great, but she wasn't going to pretend it was lucky. She'd practiced really hard to be able to play it so well. And her purse was really cute, but it had never caused anything especially cool to happen — sure, she usually had fun when she carried it, but that was because she was out with her best friends, not because of some handbag!

"Why don't I come over to your place?" Jade suggested. "I can help you pack, and I bet we'll find something lucky stashed in your room that you've completely forgotten about." Jade had had her outfits picked out for the trip for weeks now — after all, planning fabulous looks was what being a true fashionista was all about! But she knew the other girls were still trying to decide on perfect looks for a weekend at a wilderness lodge.

"I'd love to help too," Yasmin said, "but I really have to get some packing done tonight."

"Me too," Cloe added.

"No worries, girls," Jade replied. "I've totally got this covered!"

The girls split up, and twenty minutes later, Jade and Sasha were standing in the middle of Sasha's room, completely surrounded by clothes, shoes, and accessories. Checking out Sasha's entire wardrobe totally brought back memories of all the awesome outfits they'd put together for super-fun events they'd planned.

"Remember when you wore this in the fashion show?" Jade asked, holding up a shimmering, strappy red dress. Sasha had felt like a super-model in it, but she'd only worn it once, so she didn't exactly think it was lucky.

"How about this hat?" Jade suggested, tossing a leather-studded newsboy cap at Sasha as if it were a Frisbee. It had finished off Sasha's onstage look when she rocked out with the Rock Angelz.

"Or this?" she asked, holding up a halter dress with a flowery, Hawaiian print. Sasha had made a splash wearing it to their end-of-summer rooftop barbecue.

"I don't think a piece of clothing could be my good-luck charm," said Sasha. "I mean, I love all my threads, but it's not like I've won the lottery in any of them!"

"Yeah . . . ," Jade agreed, scanning the room for other possibilities. She noticed Sasha's cheerleading pom-poms lying on the floor, and scooped them up, waving them around as though she were doing a cheer herself. "What about these?" she asked. "You did lead the way to the state championship with these pom-poms!"

"Nah . . ." Sasha replied.

Jade glanced at Sasha's super-organized desk and spotted her friend's planner. "What about this?" she asked, picking up the planner. "I know you never leave home without your trusty planner, and it totally keeps your busy social schedule running smoothly."

"Yeah, but that's not luck," Sasha protested. "It's just good planning!"

"Okay, well . . . what about this?" Jade held up a pretty glass paperweight from Sasha's desk, starting to run out of ideas.

"Honestly? I have no idea where that even came from!" Sasha replied.

"Well, it looks lucky to me!" Jade declared. Both girls burst out laughing, but then Sasha collapsed on her bed, frustrated.

"I'm never going to come up with something to write about," Sasha moaned. "I think you guys better go to the mountains without me. It'll take me all weekend to put something together for this essay."

"Don't say that!" Jade cried. "Come on, we'll think of something. Who knows, maybe you'll discover your lucky charm on the trip!"

"I just don't know," Sasha replied. "This assignment really has me stumped."

"Don't give up yet!" Jade begged her friend. "C'mon, let's head to Cloe's — together. We'll get this figured out!" She flipped open her cell phone and speed-dialed Cloe to let her know they were on their way.

Chapter 2

Jade and Sasha arrived in Cloe's room to a scene of mad packing. Cloe and Yasmin had each laid out selections of puffy jackets, chic scarves, hip cargo pants, and cool patterned T-shirts on every available surface in Cloe's room.

"Wow, I feel like I'm on safari just stepping into this room," Sasha said.

Yasmin pressed. "Doesn't it make you want to head out to, I don't know, a wilderness lodge?"

"We are not going without you," Cloe added. "That is so not an option. So we'll just have to come up with something while we finish packing."

The girls tossed their weekend's ensemble of safari chic outfits into their open suitcases, then surveyed their work proudly.

"I think that just might be the fastest packing job on record," Yasmin said. "And our new out-doorsy looks are totally awesome. I can't wait to wear them!"

"Those are cute," Sasha agreed. "And I have some threads that would go perfectly with them."

"Well then you'll just have to come along and show them off," Jade declared.

"Girls, you know I want to," Sasha replied. "But I have to take care of this essay first. I need an A in this class to keep my perfect GPA!"

"Okay, what if you made up a good-luck charm?" Cloe suggested. "It is a *creative* writing class, after all — so you'll just be getting really creative!"

"But that wasn't the assignment," Sasha replied. "I just wouldn't feel right about making something up."

"Okay then, you'll just have to come along to the lodge with us to get some fresh inspiration," Yasmin announced. "You're clearly too stressed out right now. You should really come join us for some serious chill time."

"Definitely," Cloe agreed. "The great outdoors are bound to make you feel totally creative!"

"I don't know . . ." Sasha replied. "Look, I'll think about it, but for now I think I better head back to my laptop. I've got some serious thinking to do." She headed out, and the girls watched her sadly.

"This trip will be totally ruined if Sasha doesn't come!" Cloe wailed, flopping onto her bed dramatically and strewing clothes everywhere.

"Angel, it'll be okay," Jade said. "Right, Pretty Princess?" Yasmin was known to her friends as Pretty Princess because of her totally elegant, regal sense of style. But right now Yas was looking thoughtfully at the clothes on the floor.

"What is it, Yas?" Cloe asked.

"You know Sasha can't resist a hip new outfit," Yasmin began — like the rest of them, Sasha had an intense passion for fashion. "And if she had the perfect place to wear it, she definitely wouldn't want to miss that chance, right?"

"It *is* totally worth going on this trip if you get to show off an amazing new outfit," Jade agreed. "So what's the plan?"

"We'll buy Sasha a super-cool new outfit for the trip," Yasmin said, slipping on a new bright-pink jacket that made her golden hair gleam, and admiring the effect in Cloe's mirror. "When she sees it, there's no way she'll still turn down the trip!"

"On it!" Jade said. "To the mall!"

The girls jetted over to the shopping mall, one of their favorite places. They hit all the shops in a whirlwind shopping spree, and emerged with an awesome outdoorsy outfit that still captured Sasha's cool street vibe. Cloe had found a cute camo tee, and Jade added a cool green jacket. Yasmin grabbed some cropped khaki pants with pretty ribbon ties at the bottom, and a chic orange scarf that played off the jacket perfectly. Then Jade found some hip sneakers with green and orange stripes, and Cloe picked out a slouchy corduroy bag that was just big enough for the essentials — bottled water, granola bars, and of course lip gloss!

"Perfect!" Cloe declared.

"Ooh, we should grab some of that makeup," Jade said, pointing at the window of Make-up Mirror. Some of the season's hottest eye-shadow colors were in cool shades drawn from nature, like golden green, khaki, and brown. "Those colors would really bring out Sasha's eyes, plus they totally match this new outfit!"

They headed into the store, and Cloe grabbed a tube of waterproof mascara. "We'll need this when we go canoeing," she said, thinking Jade was right behind her. Instead, another voice responded.

"Canoeing, eh?" said a nasal voice. Cloe spun around and saw Kirstee and Kaycee, two of the meanest girls at Stiles High. The twin sisters' evil deeds had earned them the nickname the Tweevils.

"What's it to you?" asked Cloe coolly.

"Don't tell me you fashion freaks are going back to nature," said Kirstee. She was the smarter of the two girls, and the one who dreamed up most of their vicious schemes. "What a joke!" she said.

"Hey, wouldn't this lip gloss look amazing on Sasha —" said Yasmin, coming up to Cloe. She stopped abruptly when she saw the Tweevils. They were definitely up to no good.

"When is this trip to the great outdoors?" asked Kaycee.

"Why do you care?" Jade asked suspiciously, motioning to Yasmin and Cloe that it was time to go. "You don't exactly strike me as nature-lovers."

"We are too!" Kaycee screeched. The girls rolled their eyes and headed for the door, but Kirstee blocked their way.

"We hope this little nature retreat isn't taking place at the Misty Mountain Lodge," she said. "Kaycee and I have booked a room there this weekend, and we'd like to avoid both gnats and Bratz."

Yasmin, Cloe, and Jade looked at each other in horror. How'd they get unlucky enough to have the Tweevils booked at the same lodge on the same weekend?

"No worries," said Yasmin. "It's a big lodge."

"And I'm sure we'll find things to do that wouldn't exactly interest you," Jade added.

"Know what would interest me?" Kirstee asked. "Scoping out your nature trail fashion show. I'm sure your idea of hiking gear is hilarious!"

"Oh and yours isn't?" Jade snapped. "I'm sorry, I didn't know they made hiking boots in pink." The Tweevils thought anything pink was the height of fashion, and were never seen in any other color.

"Of course they do!" Kaycee exclaimed. "We just bought matching pairs!"

"Sounds great," Yasmin muttered, as she and the girls hurried out of the store, leaving their makeup finds behind. Getting away from the Tweevils was more important even than snagging new products.

"Bye, Nature Girls," Kirstee taunted the girls as they left. "See you in the mountains!"

"Not if we see you first," Jade said under her breath as they headed out of the mall.

"This is terrible!" Cloe cried. "Those meanies are going to ruin our whole weekend!"

"No way," said Yasmin. "We just won't let them. And besides, it really *is* a big lodge. There's no reason we should have to see them up there." But she was still worried. Wherever the Tweevils went, they seemed to bring trouble, and she'd been hoping for a totally relaxing weekend!

A few minutes later, the Bratz showed up at Sasha's house, loaded down with shopping bags. When they saw the look of surprise on Sasha's face as she flung open the door, they forgot all about their Tweevil troubles.

"What's all this?" Sasha asked, pointing to the shopping bags.

"Your new outfit for the mountains," Jade

replied. "Now hurry up and try it on — the suspense is killing us!"

"But —" Sasha began.

"Oh, I'm sorry," Cloe said sweetly. "That wasn't actually a question." The girls laughed as Sasha led the way to her bedroom, where they unveiled her amazing new outfit.

"This is for me?" Sasha asked, touching the soft fleece of the jacket.

"You bet," said Cloe. "We promise to help you with your essay, Bunny Boo. But you have to help us have the coolest vacation ever!"

Sasha smiled at her best friends. With friends like these, she knew she'd figure out her essay issues in no time. Maybe they were right — a weekend away might be just the thing to get her creative juices flowing.

"Okay, guys," Sasha said. "You talked me into it. But now you have to help me finish packing — I can't wear just one outfit all weekend, no matter how cool it is!"

"Yay!" the girls cheered, pulling Sasha into a group hug.

"This is going to be one super-fun weekend," Jade said happily.

"If the Tweevils don't ruin it," Yasmin said glumly. They explained to Sasha about running into the Tweevils at the mall, and she pursed her lips worriedly.

"Now I definitely have to come — I'll protect you from those evil Tweevils!" she announced. The others laughed, then gathered around a Misty Mountain Lodge brochure to plan the perfect getaway.

Chapter 3

"Misty Mountain Lodge, here we come!" Cloe yelled happily.

School had just let out for the weekend, and the girls had hopped into Cloe's cruiser as soon as the bell rang. Their luggage was already stashed in the back so they could get on the road right away. Everyone was buzzing with excitement.

"Here's to three days of livin' it up!" said Yasmin, clinking her bottle of water with Jade's.

In ten minutes, the girls were cruising down the highway, singing along to their favorite tunes. Yasmin painted her nails a pretty pink, while Jade sketched new fashion ideas in her zebra-print notebook. Sasha, in the front, was manning the radio, surfing the stations to keep the cool grooves coming. The girls couldn't have been happier.

It was late afternoon when they pulled into the lodge, a rustic stone building nestled in woods at the top of a mountain. "What an awesome view!" cried Sasha, checking out the lush valley that stretched below the lodge. She was so glad her friends had talked her into joining them!

Cloe was happy to see that the lodge was as beautiful as the photo in the brochure. The lobby was charming and cozy, with a large stone fire-place. The girls helped themselves to apple cider and freshly-baked chocolate chip cookies, still warm from the oven, as they checked in.

"I'm totally down with the homemade cookies," said Jade. "Come on, let's check out the room."

Their suite was totally adorable, with gorgeous quilts on the bed and an old-fashioned weather vane hanging on the wall. Through the window, they had a spectacular view of the mountains.

Cloe opened the window and took a deep breath. "Mmm, I love that mountain air!" she said.

"Well let's get out there!" Sasha suggested. "Anyone up for a little canoeing?"

"Count me in!" exclaimed Cloe. She thought canoeing was fun! Yasmin and Jade decided to check out some hiking trails, after scoping out the lodge's boutique, of course. They unzipped their suitcases, excited to try on their new clothes.

Cloe threw on a green baby tee, waterproof camouflage-patterned pants, and a vintage baseball cap. Sasha paired some khaki cargo pants with a black hoodie over a white tank top. Sure, they were getting back to nature, but who said you couldn't do it in style?

After getting directions from the lodge, Sasha and Cloe followed the trail down to the water and found a fleet of canoes waiting on the riverbank. "Let's take this one," said Cloe, pointing to a silver one. "It's the prettiest one."

"And it *is* important to have a pretty canoe," Sasha teased.

"Obviously!" Cloe replied, grinning.

As she stepped into the water, Sasha almost lost her balance. The current was swifter than she'd realized. She and Cloe fastened their life jackets, looking up at the breathtaking scenery.

"Can you believe we were in math class just a few short hours ago?" Cloe asked.

"I have to say, this is definitely better!" Sasha replied. The girls climbed into their canoe, and soon the fast-moving water had carried them away.

With smooth strokes, the girls guided the canoe around some small rocks, until Sasha spotted some serious rapids up ahead. "Ooh, we better be careful up there," she said.

Cloe squinted and back-paddled to slow the boat down. "Yeah, looks like we're in for some white-water rafting," she said. "But I think if we keep toward the right, we should be able to avoid it."

But as they approached the fast-moving water, the canoe got harder to control. "Yikes!" cried Sasha. Suddenly, the boat lurched forward, and the girls were thrown into the water.

Gasping for air, they tried to swim toward the riverbank, but the water was strong. Opening her eyes, Sasha saw a pair of tanned arms reach for her — but those didn't look like Cloe's arms!

"Wha — ?" she gasped, between gulps of water.

The arms lifted her onto the riverbank, and when Sasha wiped the water away from her eyes, she saw a tall, cute guy in a wetsuit standing in front of her. He smiled down at her, and she couldn't help smiling back as she took in his big blue eyes and sandy sun-streaked hair. "I'm Skye," he said, "and this is Topher."

A few feet away, a guy with brown hair and a golden tan was placing Cloe on the shore. Hearing his name, the other guy caught Sasha's eye and waved. "We're staying at the lodge," Skye explained. "We were kayaking and saw your canoe tip over."

"Well, we're glad you did," said Cloe, wiping her face off with a bandanna. "You're our heroes!" She looked up into Topher's big green eyes and thought *These guys are really cute.*

"All in a day's work," said Topher, grinning. "We're here with our outdoor adventure club. Maybe you'd want to come out on a hike or something with us later this weekend?" He passed a bottle of water to Cloe and handed Sasha a towel.

"Yeah, the guys are great, but having a few girls around would be cool, too," Skye added.

"That sounds awesome," Cloe said.

"Actually, our club is having a party at the lodge tomorrow night for St. Patrick's Day," said Topher. "How would you two like to be our guests?"

Cloe and Sasha looked at each other excitedly, feeling fully recovered from their canoeing mishap. "Definitely," Sasha replied.

"But only if we can bring our friends Yasmin and Jade," Cloe added.

"The more the merrier," said Skye.

The boys helped them drag their canoe back to shore, and then the four of them hung out on the riverbank for awhile, sharing energy bars and talking about school, sports, and travel. But soon Cloe glanced at her waterproof watch and exclaimed, "Oh man, we've gotta run. We're supposed to meet Yasmin and Jade for dinner."

"We'll slip the invitation under your door," promised Skye. "What's your room number?"

"One-oh-seven," said Sasha. She laughed when Skye took out a pen and wrote it on the inside of his arm. "Now I can't forget it," he said.

Sasha pulled Cloe to her feet and they ran up the trail to the lodge, waving back at the boys. They couldn't wait to tell Yasmin and Cloe about the cool guys they'd met — and the awesome party invitation! They just hoped they'd packed something cute enough for a party, in with all their outdoor adventure clothes.

Cloe couldn't stop smiling. They'd only been here for a few hours, and already it had been an amazing trip. She couldn't imagine what cool things were in store for the rest of the weekend!

Chapter 4

Walking along the mountain trail, Yasmin and Jade closed their eyes and inhaled the clean, pine-scented air. After climbing up a steep, winding trail, they oohed and aahed at the dramatic view of the mountain range.

"Is this awesome, or what?" asked Jade.

Yasmin nodded, taking in the lush valley ringed by violet mountains. She leaned down to pick a bright pink wildflower, sniffed it, and tucked it into her hatband. This hike had been so refreshing. She hoped Cloe and Sasha were having as much fun as they were.

"I just feel so lucky to be here," said Yasmin. She bent down and picked a couple of clovers, twisting them together and plucking a couple of leaves to create a fake four-leaf clover.

"This is for you," she said, handing the clover to Jade. "It's your lucky four-leaf clover."

Jade accepted the clover, twirling the stem between her fingers thoughtfully. "I wish it were that easy to create a good-luck charm for Sasha."

Yasmin thought a moment. "Maybe it is," she said. "This weekend, let's show her there's good luck in the world — everywhere you look."

"How will we do that?" Jade asked. "I mean, I think it would take a leprechaun showing up in our room and personally handing Sasha his pot of gold for her to believe in luck!"

"That's it!" Yasmin squealed.

"Um, Yas, do you have a pot of gold I don't know about?" Jade asked.

"No," Yasmin said. "But I do know a couple of leprechauns!"

"Sweetie, I think the mountain air has gotten to you," Jade said. "Let's get you back to the room so you can come back to your senses."

"No, I'm serious!" Yasmin replied. "We'll be Sasha's lucky leprechauns! We'll leave her good-luck charms all weekend. Then she's bound to end up with something to write her essay about!"

Jade considered this. The mountains were full of wildflowers and birds' nests, but short on cool stuff to buy. "And where will we get these lucky charms?" she asked.

"The lodge gift shop!" declared Yasmin. "I bet they have tons of cool stuff."

"Well, I never pass up a shopping trip," said Jade. "Especially if it's for a good cause."

"Definitely," said Yasmin. The girls high-fived each other, then Jade tossed the four-leaf clover over the guardrail. "Here's to good luck!" said Jade.

As they made their way down the winding trail, Yasmin and Jade chatted about their plan. They could leave a good-luck charm on Sasha's pillow, or inside one of her jacket pockets. "How about right on top of her hairbrush?" suggested Jade. This was going to be fun.

When they came to a fork in the trail, they were puzzled. "I don't remember this fork," Yasmin said. "Which way are we supposed to go?"

"I don't know," said Jade, looking at the thick forest. "Let's try this way and see what happens." As they headed down the path, they came upon a stream with a log across it.

"I know we haven't seen that stream before," said Yasmin. "Let's retrace our steps." They trudged back up the trail, trying to find the fork in the road, but now there was another split in the trail that led in three different directions. They were completely confused.

"Are you thinking what I'm thinking?" asked Jade. "We're lost!"

Yasmin tried not to panic. The afternoon sun was growing dimmer now, and soon it would be dinnertime. Where were all the other hikers?

"Let's just choose one of these paths and hope for the best," said Yasmin briskly. "We'll probably run into other people eventually."

They started on one of the downhill trails, following its many twists and turns. Again, they ended up at the log covering the bubbling stream. They had gone in a big circle.

"Okay, now I'm officially worried," admitted Yasmin.

Just then, they heard footsteps and the rustle of leaves as people pushed through them. "Look who's here!" said a nasal voice. Yasmin and Jade looked at each other — they knew that voice. It was Kaycee!

"Looking for the rest of the Bratz pack?" asked Kirstee. "We'll show you how to get back to the lodge if you give us something. How about your hat?" she asked, pointing to Yasmin's green hat with the wildflower tucked into it.

"Or your backpack," said Kaycee, eyeing Jade's eye-catching khaki messenger bag trimmed in black.

"No way!" said Jade. "We're just enjoying our hike — we don't need your help!"

"Suit yourself!" sniffed Kirstee. "We don't want any of your stupid stuff anyway."

Kirstee and Kaycee scampered away down a trail, and Yasmin and Jade looked at each other. "No way was I going to let those jerks bully us," said Jade.

"Me either," said Yasmin. "But, well . . . how are we going to get back?"

"Did you see Kirstee's backpack?" asked Yasmin. "One of her keychains has a bell on it. You can hear it in the distance." Jade heard a faint tinkling.

"Follow that bell," said Yasmin. "But let's stay far enough behind them so they don't notice us. I mean, we don't want them to think we're just trying to tag along!"

Jade and Yasmin followed the sound of the bell through the woods and, sure enough, the trail led them back to the lodge.

The girls hurried inside and bolted across the lobby to the gift shop, hoping it was still open.

"It closes in twenty minutes," reported Jade, checking the sign on the window. "We'll have to move fast."

The Bratz loved a shopping challenge. "How cute is this?" asked Jade, picking up a miniature bamboo plant in a pretty painted pot. Yasmin scanned the jewelry case. "I'm loving this wishbone pendant," she said, holding up a necklace with a silver charm. It was totally hip — exactly Sasha's style.

"These things will make fantastic lucky charms for Sasha," said Jade, browsing through a rack of silver wind chimes. "Maybe she really *will* think they were brought by a leprechaun."

On the other side of the rack, Kirstee's ears perked up. She and Kaycee had also stopped into the gift shop after their hike. When Kirstee spotted Yasmin and Jade, she dragged her twin behind a display of sweaters. She craned her neck, trying to overhear their conversation from her hiding place.

"Why are we . . . ?" began Kaycee.

"Shhhhhhhh," said Kirstee, putting her hand over her sister's mouth. She strained to hear more. Yasmin and Jade were buying lucky charms to leave secretly for Sasha? *Fascinating.*

When the Bratz left the gift shop, Kirstee removed her hand from Kaycee's mouth and hurried upstairs with her sister. Once they were in their room, she explained her plan to Kaycee. If lucky charms were the Bratz girls' new game, she was definitely ready to play. She thought she just might have to leave Sasha a little charm of her own . . .

Chapter 5

When Yasmin and Jade got back to the room, Sasha and Cloe were bursting with excitement.

"We had the greatest afternoon!" said Cloe, removing her dripping wet jacket. "You'll never believe what happened —"

Sasha was combing tangles out of her soaking wet hair. "If only you guys had been with us," she said breathlessly. Her clothes were completely drenched, but she didn't look upset about it.

"Hey, hey, hey — slow down!" said Jade, laughing at her friends' excitement. "What happened?"

"We were going down the river in this canoe —" Sasha began. "It looked peaceful at first, but the water was moving fast —"

"Suddenly we hit some rapids and . . . major wipeout!" Cloe said, dramatically throwing her hands in the air.

"The canoe tipped over and threw us into the river!" exclaimed Sasha. She reported this story as though she was thrilled by the outcome. She peeled off her wet pants.

"And that was a *good* thing?" Jade asked doubtfully, exchanging glances with Yasmin. "Sorry, girls — but I'm not getting it."

Cloe and Sasha looked at each other and laughed. "Well, it wasn't a good thing at first," said Sasha. "I felt like a sock being spun around in a washing machine. But suddenly this hand reached out and pulled me out of the water."

"These two guys appeared out of nowhere and rescued us," explained Cloe. "They were so nice and helpful and —"

"Super-cute," Sasha interjected. "Their names are Topher and Skye. They belong to this outdoor adventure club that's staying here at the lodge this weekend. And the best part is —"

"They invited us to a party on Saturday night!" Cloe announced, delivering the news with relish. "Isn't that awesome?" After she had discarded her wet clothes in a pile, she stepped into a bathrobe provided by the lodge, and smoothed some vanilla body lotion onto her arms.

Jade and Yasmin looked at each other happily — that *was* good news!

"Where did you guys go on your hike?" asked Cloe. "Did you meet anyone?"

Jade pretended to pout. "Yeah, we met people all right. Some people you already know . . ."

"It's unfair," protested Yasmin. "You ran into some really nice guys, and we ran into . . ."

Cloe and Sasha looked at each other, their eyes wide.

"The Tweevils!" shouted Jade, unable to keep it in.

"Oh no," said Cloe. "I was hoping they were bluffing when they said they were coming here. Talk about spoiling your appetite."

"Tell me about it," said Yasmin. "I hope that's the last we see of them."

After Cloe and Sasha changed clothes, they continued their gabfest over dinner at the lodge's restaurant. There were some important issues to discuss, like what to wear to the big party. After a spirited debate about whether to go glam or casual, they raised their sodas in a toast.

"Here's to adventure, nature, fashion, and —" Cloe started.

"Friends!" added Jade.

The girls clinked their glasses and gulped down their sodas. All through dinner they continued the party wardrobe debate: ruffled mini-skirt or cargo pants? Up-dos or long 'n' luscious locks? They did know one thing: on Saturday night they *had* to look fabulous.

When they got back to the room, they were tired but happy, and definitely looking forward to the next day. Sasha sank onto her bed with a thump. "Hey, what's this?" she asked, feeling something hard on her pillow.

Pulling back the cover, she found the wishbone pendant. "It's . . . beautiful," she said, examining the silver charm. "What is it?"

"Looks like a good-luck charm to me," said Jade, winking at Cloe.

Sasha rolled her eyes. Good-luck charms were wishful thinking, but she fastened the necklace around her neck anyway. The delicate silver chain looked great with her tailored white shirt.

"Okay, guys," said Sasha. "'Fess up . . . Who do I have to thank for this awesome accessory?"

Jade and Yasmin busied themselves with unpacking their suitcases and pretended not to hear. "Don't look at *me*," said Cloe.

Sasha shrugged and headed into the bathroom. Once she shut the door, Cloe turned to Jade and Yasmin questioningly. Jade started to explain, but then Sasha reappeared. "I'm beat," she announced, pulling back the covers to her bed.

Sasha pulled on some flannel pajamas printed with a pattern of tiny polka dots. Even at bedtime, Sasha looked totally chic. She gathered her hair up in a ponytail and yawned.

"So, no one's claiming credit for this gorgeous

gift?" said Sasha as she climbed into bed. She ran her fingers over the pendant. It really was beautiful.

"Maybe you shouldn't rule out a leprechaun friend," said Jade, looking at Yasmin. "Aren't the mountains supposed to be full of woodland spirits? Remember that mythology unit we had in English class last year —"

But Sasha's eyes were closed, and her breathing had gotten shallow. She had fallen asleep with her necklace on, her lips curled into a faint smile. *Probably dreaming about one of those cute guys they met*, thought Yasmin.

Jade walked over to Sasha's bed to make sure she was really asleep. "Thanks for giving me your new suede jacket," she whispered mischievously. When she got no response, Jade knew she was out cold.

Cloe glanced at Sasha, then pulled Jade and

Yasmin into the hallway. "Okay, girls. You can tell me. Have you guys been playing leprechaun?"

"You caught us," Yasmin admitted. "But don't tell Sasha!"

"We decided to slip her a few good-luck charms," added Jade. "We figure if anything will make her believe in good luck, that will!"

Cloe looked at them thoughtfully. "I'm in," she said. "And you know, meeting those guys today was totally good luck. Maybe it'll make a believer out of Sasha, after all."

All three girls snuck back into the room and peered down at their blissfully sleeping friend. "Stay tuned," whispered Yasmin. "The good luck is just beginning."

The Bratz were so busy planning their leprechaun schemes, they didn't hear the sound of something being left outside their door. The Tweevils, however, noticed it right away when they passed the girls' room late that night.

"Kaycee, look!" said Kirstee. "In front of Room one-oh-seven."

"That's where the Bratz are staying, right?" said Kaycee. She stooped down to examine the delivery. It was a single yellow rose wrapped in clear cellophane, with a red satin ribbon tied around its stem. Tucked into the ribbon was an envelope addressed To SASHA AND CLOE.

"Of course it's their suite," snarled Kirstee. "Now go snatch that flower and envelope and slip it into your purse."

Kaycee hesitated, looking both ways down the hall.

"Well, don't just stand there!" said Kirstee, disgusted by her sister's hesitation. She swiped the package herself, and the Tweevils raced back to their room.

Perched on her bed, Kirstee tore open the envelope. "'You are invited to the Woodridge High School Outdoor Adventure Club's annual St. Patrick's Day bash,'" she read.

"It's Saturday night at nine, in the main hall," Kaycee said. She looked at her sister. "I'm glad *we* found this before the Bratz did," she said.

Kirstee smiled in satisfaction. A party like that would probably be packed with boys! And swiping the invite meant they'd get to go, while the Bratz girls definitely would not!

Score one for the twins, she thought. She unwrapped the rose and held it under her nose, inhaling its sweet scent.

So far this was shaping up to be an excellent weekend, she thought mischievously.

Chapter 6

The next morning, Cloe was the first to wake up. She pulled up the window shade and peered out at the mountains dappled with morning sunlight. It was going to be a gorgeous day.

Looking around, she saw that her friends were still sleeping. Since she was already awake, she decided to head out for a quick morning run. Moving quietly to avoid disturbing the others, Cloe slipped on her track pants and a T-shirt.

At the door, she checked for the invitation the boys had promised to drop off, but there was nothing there. She sighed, trying not to be disappointed. She was sure they'd drop it off sometime during the day.

She jogged down to the lobby and stepped out into the cool mountain air, immediately forgetting about anything but her totally spectacular surroundings.

The rest of the girls woke up gradually, enjoying a lazy morning. Yasmin went to the window and pulled up the shade the rest of the way. "Horseback riding, anyone?" she asked. Jade and Sasha nodded enthusiastically. That would be the perfect way to check out the scenery — plus they all totally loved animals.

The girls pulled on jeans, T-shirts, and zip-up hoodie sweatshirts. "Hold on, girls," said Jade. "I have the perfect accessory." From her suitcase she pulled out a bouquet of bandannas, all in delicious bright colors. "I call orange!" cried Sasha, grabbing the bright-orange one and tying it around her waist like a belt.

Jade took the green one, which matched her eyes perfectly. She twisted it into a headband, which look awesome against her glossy black hair. Yasmin selected the hot-pink one, and tied it around her shiny brown ponytail. "Now we look like real cowgirls!" she declared.

After a quick breakfast of apricot-walnut granola and yogurt, the girls set out for the stable. Inside the stone building, a white-haired man in a cowboy hat greeted them warmly.

"I'm Mr. Dooley," he said. "We'll set up you ladies with some horses."

"Hey, Cody," Mr. Dooley called out. A tanned

boy with dark hair and bright blue eyes appeared and shook hands with the girls. "Cute!" Sasha whispered to Yasmin.

Cody headed into the horse stalls and returned with a gorgeous honey-colored horse. "This is Butterscotch," he said, helping Sasha into the saddle. Sasha noticed that Cody's eyelashes were long and pretty, like the horse's.

"Whoa, horsy!" cried Sasha, as Butterscotch started to whinny. Cody stroked the horse's nose and fed him a sugar cube. Next, he brought out a striking white horse named Snowball and helped Jade climb on.

Yasmin inhaled the delicious scent of hay while she waited for her horse to be led out. Looking around the stable, her eyes hit upon a black horseshoe mounted on the wall. *Now that would make a perfect good-luck charm*, she thought.

"Hey Mr. Dooley," Yasmin asked quietly, trying

not to attract the other girls' attention. "Do you happen to have a spare horseshoe?"

"Sure," he said. He ducked into the tack room and emerged with a shiny silver horseshoe. "Will this do?"

"That's perfect!" she said, stuffing it into her khaki messenger bag. "Thank you so much!"

Outside, Cody was waiting with a beautiful brown horse. "This is autumn," he said, giving Yasmin a leg up into the saddle.

"That's perfect for you, Pretty Princess," said Jade. "Her favorite season," she explained to Cody.

"Mine too," he said with a smile.

Then Cody hopped onto his own horse, a caramel-colored beauty that he introduced as Pumpkin. "Stay in a line behind me," he told the girls. He led them out on a winding trail along a mountain ridge.

Easier said than done, thought Sasha. Her horse, Butterscotch, had a mind of its own. The horse kept wandering off to the side, trying to eat the grass that grew along the trail.

"Stop that!" Sasha cried.

"Just grab the reins firmly and guide him back to the path," Cody called out.

But Butterscotch seemed determined to take his own path. He started trotting along in a different direction, ignoring Sasha's tugs on the reins. She held on tightly until Butterscotch came to an abrupt stop, facing another group of horses on a trail ride.

"Well, well, well, look who's here!" Sasha heard a familiar nasal voice and looked up. Kirstee and Kaycee were riding by on identical black horses. "Having a little trouble there?" Kaycee asked with a smirk, looking at Butterscotch.

"Even the horse is terrified by her fashion disasters," sneered Kirstee, staring at Sasha's bandana.

Just then, the others rode up behind Sasha. "Don't listen to them, Sasha," said Jade. "You did great with Butterscotch."

"Sorry Butterscotch got a little spooked," Cody added, riding up beside Sasha. "Are you okay?" Sasha nodded, and the Tweevils glared at her, annoyed that she had the cute guide's full attention.

"Listen," Kirstee interrupted. "We just want to wish you guys *good luck*."

"Especially Sasha . . . she'll need it!" With that, she and Kirstee looked at each other and burst out in laughter before riding off to follow their own guide.

Sasha, Jade, and Yasmin looked at each other. Did the Tweevils know something about their secret plan for the weekend?

"Those chicks are total weirdos," said Jade, shaking her head.

The girls brought their horses back into line and continued their ride up the mountain. Even Butterscotch behaved himself for the rest of the ride. Cody pointed out some perfect spots to get spectacular views of the valley. At the end of the ride, the girls patted their horses' noses and thanked them for a great ride, then waved good-bye to Cody and Mr. Dooley.

"What a great ride," sighed Sasha. "Even if my horse did freak out and lead me straight to the Tweevils." She hoisted her dark-green mini-backpack over her shoulder.

Why does this bag feel so heavy? Sasha wondered, trying to remember what was in it. She started rummaging through its contents: peppermint hand lotion, cell phone, sunglasses. Suddenly her hand hit upon something hard she didn't recognize.

"Hey!" she said, pulling out an iron horseshoe. "What's this?"

Yasmin put on an innocent face. She had slipped the horseshoe into Sasha's bag while her friend grabbed a drink of water back at the stable. "Another good-luck charm?" she suggested. She and Jade exchanged glances. "I think you may have attracted your very own leprechaun, just in time for St. Patrick's Day," teased Jade, who figured Yasmin had planted the horseshoe in Sasha's bag.

"Yeah, right," said Sasha. Maybe the horseshoe had somehow fallen into her bag back at the stables. Either that, or someone was trying awfully hard to shower her with good luck.

Walking into the lodge, the girls ran into Cloe. "Hey, Angel," Jade said. "Did Topher and Skye ever drop off that party invitation?"

"No," said Cloe. "And I know Skye had our room number because he wrote it on his arm." Seeing the other girls' disappointed faces, Cloe tried to reassure them. "Maybe they just forgot. I'm going for a hike around the lake. I'm sure it will turn up later."

"I'll join you," Jade said, as the others headed back to the lodge.

As she trekked up to their room, Sasha couldn't shake the feeling that something strange was going on. The Tweevils' strange remarks, these good-luck charms that kept magically appearing, and the missing invitation all seemed a little off to her. *But what could it all mean?* she wondered.

Chapter 7

When the girls got back to the room, the invitation was nowhere to be found. Instead, there was a tiny package at their door, wrapped in silver paper and tied with a green satin ribbon. Attached to the ribbon was a gift tag that read To Sasha.

Yasmin was puzzled — she knew Jade hadn't left anything this morning. And she had left the lucky bamboo on Sasha's dresser, but Sasha hadn't found it yet. But then she realized Cloe must have decided to get in on the act while they were off on their trail ride.

Sasha grabbed the gift and carried it into their room. Inside, she tore off the wrapping paper to reveal a pretty tube labeled SUPER DELUXE HAIR MASCARA.

"I can't wait to try this out!" she said happily.

Yasmin grinned at her friend, sure that this was Cloe's little gift. She wasn't exactly sure how hair mascara was supposed to tie into the good-luck theme, but Sasha certainly seemed happy with it, and that was definitely all that mattered.

"This is awesome," said Sasha. "You guys really outdid yourselves at finding presents I'd totally love."

"We had nothing to do with this," Yasmin protested.

"Sure you didn't," Sasha said with a wink. "I'm sure it's some woodland leprechaun who knows exactly what I'd like. That definitely makes more sense than it just being you girls."

Then she noticed the lucky bamboo perched on her dresser. "Is this for me too?" she gasped. "You girls are out of control!"

Yasmin didn't say anything as Sasha hurried into the bathroom to try out her new hair mascara. Yasmin stretched on the bed and jotted some story ideas in her notebook, happy to have some time for her writing.

Cloe squeezed sunscreen onto her palm and rubbed it onto her face, then handed the tube to Jade. A hike around the lake was sure to chill them out, and give them time to brainstorm more ideas to convince Sasha that there was really luck in the air.

"Do you think we could find an actual four-leaf clover?" Jade asked.

"Maybe . . ." Cloe said. "Or maybe we can just get her a four-leaf-clover bracelet. I think I saw one in the gift shop."

Just then, the girls saw the backs of two guys at the top of the hill, one with blonde hair and one with dark hair.

"That's Topher and Skye!" Cloe whispered excitedly to Jade as they hurried up the path.

"Hey, guys!" Cloe called. The guys seemed to be absorbed in a conversation, but they turned around and waved at her.

As she approached, she heard other voices. "We don't really like the outdoors much," a female voice was saying. "But we were so bored at home, we thought we'd try a weekend in the mountains."

That's Kaycee, Cloe realized. She'd recognize that annoying voice anywhere. She felt bad for the boys, being stuck with the Tweevils. But then she realized — if Topher and Skye knew the Tweevils, then it was no wonder the party invitation had never arrived. The Tweevils had probably said lots of awful things about the Bratz, and the boys had decided not to invite them after all.

Cloe stopped in her tracks, realizing she really didn't want to join this foursome. "What's wrong, Angel?" Jade asked. "Aren't you going to introduce me?"

"Jade, you're right, we have to get back to the lodge!" she said loudly. "See you later, guys!" With that, she grabbed Jade's wrist and bolted down the hill as the boys stared after them, confused.

"What is going on?" Jade asked when they reached a clearing and Cloe finally stopped power-walking.

"Don't you get it?" Cloe demanded. "The Tweevils

met our new friends, and totally corrupted them. I'm sure they talked the guys into not inviting us to the party."

"Do you really think they would do that?" Jade asked. Cloe shot her a look, and Jade nodded. "Yeah, they're the Tweevils — of course they would."

"I just don't know how we'll break it to the others," Cloe said sadly.

They were heading toward the lodge when Cloe felt a tap on her shoulder. She spun around. "Topher!" she cried. "What are you doing here?"

"What happened?" he asked. "We were so happy to run into you again, and then you just took off."

"I . . . you were?" Cloe sputtered. She had been so sure that Kaycee had turned the boys against them.

"Totally," he said. "I told Skye I'd track you

66

down." He noticed Jade and added, "So, who's your friend?"

"Hi, I'm Jade," Jade said, holding out her hand. "And I take it you're Topher?"

"Sure am," he replied. "It's great to meet you!" Then he turned back to Cloe and asked, "Hey, did you get the party invitation I dropped by?"

"No," Cloe replied. "I thought maybe you forgot."

"Are you kidding? I've told everyone in the club about you girls!" Topher insisted. "I can't believe you didn't get the invitation. Room one-oh-seven, right?"

He pointed to his arm, where he had written the number in ballpoint pen. The writing was faded but still readable. "We dropped it off last night because we wanted you to get it right away."

Cloe shook her head.

"We attached it to a long-stemmed rose and left

it at your door," he said. Suddenly, he seemed shy. "The rose was Skye's idea," he added.

"Aw, that's so sweet!" Cloe said. "But we never got it."

"Well then, it's a good thing we ran into you," Topher said. "Here, I think I have an extra one in my jacket." He rummaged around in his pocket and finally pulled out an invite. "Better late than never, right?" he asked as he held it out to Cloe.

"Now promise you'll be there," he said. Turning to Jade, he added, "Both of you."

"Try to stop us!" Jade said, as Cloe tucked the invite into her backpack.

As they chatted with Topher, Cloe tried to figure out who could possibly have stolen their invitation. The lodge seemed like a safe place, and that was such a strange thing to snatch.

Just then, the Tweevils strolled by. *Ah-ha*, thought Cloe. "Hey, Topher!" Kirstee cooed. As she walked by, Cloe noticed a yellow rose in the buttonhole of her denim jacket.

"Topher," Cloe began. "Was the rose you dropped off yellow, by any chance?" she asked.

"Yeah," Topher said. "How did you know?"

"Just a lucky guess," she said. "We'll see you tonight, okay? Right now, we've got to meet up with our friends." She linked her arm through Jade's and steered her toward the lodge.

"Now what?" Jade asked.

"I'll explain inside," Cloe promised.

Chapter 8

"So what do you think happened to the invite?"

"The Tweevils took it," Cloe said grimly. "Did you see that yellow rose Kirstee was wearing?"

"Yeah," Jade said. "Not exactly my style."

"Jade, the point is, that had to be the rose that the boys attached to the invitation," Cloe explained.

"Ohmigosh, what is wrong with those girls?" Jade asked.

"I don't know, but they aren't going to get away with it," Cloe declared.

"I heard Kaycee say something about the hot tub while you were talking to Topher," Jade said. "Come on, let's get those tricky Tweevils!"

"I think I saw them go into the Jacuzzi," said Jade. "Follow me."

The hot tub was in a glass enclosure, overlooking the mountains on three sides.

"What are you girls doing here?" asked Kirstee. "Can't you see the hot tub's taken?"

"Oh, we're not here to join you," said Jade. "We just want you to return the party invitation you stole from us."

"Party invitation? You're confusing me with someone who cares," said Kirstee, hiding her annoyance. She'd hoped to keep the freaky foursome away from the bash so she and her sister would have all the boys to themselves.

"Yeah, we didn't steal that party invitation, *or* your stupid rose," Kaycee chimed in.

"Shut *up*, Kaycee," Kirstee said.

"It's okay, it's not like we didn't know it was you," Cloe said. "Topher told me he delivered a yellow rose to our door attached to an invite. Kind of like this one . . ." Cloe plucked the rose out of Kirstee's denim jacket, which was draped over her backpack in the corner of the room.

"Kirstee, you are *so* busted!" Kaycee exclaimed.

"I could've bought that myself at the lodge shop," Kirstee pointed out. "You haven't proved anything."

"I guess we'll know when you show up at the party tonight," said Jade. "Because I have a feeling the guys will be very surprised to see you there." With that, she turned on her heel, and she and Cloe strode out of the room.

When they were alone again, Kaycee looked at Kirstee. "I told you we'd get in trouble."

"Oh, stop it," said Kirstee impatiently. "Getting yelled at by that pair of fashion misfits is funny, not scary. Pull yourself together. We're about to have those Bratz exactly where we want them."

Cloe and Jade headed for the lodge, laughing at how shocked the Tweevils had been that they'd gotten caught. Suddenly, they heard footsteps behind them. Two pairs of hands grabbed their shirts and whirled them around.

"Hey!" shrieked Jade. "This is a brand-new shirt!"

"Then maybe you still have time to get your money back," Kirstee said spitefully.

"Didn't you girls get enough already?" Cloe asked.

"Not quite yet," Kirstee replied. "We just thought you might like to know that you aren't the only ones playing leprechaun this weekend."

Jade and Cloe looked at each other. What was *that* supposed to mean? And how did the Tweevils know about their scheme to help Sasha?

"Meaning?" Jade demanded.

"Meaning we've left your friend a little good-luck charm ourselves," said Kaycee.

"She's probably trying it out right now," said Kirstee. "And we'll all get to laugh at the results tonight."

Giggling evilly, the Tweevils stalked off, leaving Cloe and Jade staring at each other in dismay.

"We have to get to Sasha before whatever those mean girls left gets to her," Cloe cried. They booked it back into the lodge, determined to rescue their friend.

But as soon as they reached their room, they

knew they were too late. They heard Sasha wailing from the bathroom, "It's *terrible!* I can never come out again!" while Yasmin tried to calm her down through the door.

"What happened?" Jade asked.

"I'm not sure," Yasmin replied. "When we came back to the room, there was a present waiting for Sasha. It was this brand of hair mascara she'd been wanting to try, so she went to put it on."

"Oh, no!" Cloe cried.

"Didn't you get that for her?" Yasmin asked.

"No, the Tweevils did!" Cloe replied. She explained what had happened as Yasmin shook her head, amazed that anyone could be so mean.

"So what do you think it did to Sasha's hair?" Jade asked. The girls just shook their heads — there was no limit to what those Tweevils might try.

Chapter 9

Cloe and Jade pounded on the door. "Hey Sasha, it's us — open up!" No response. They pounded harder. "Sasha, come on. Let us in!" Cloe begged.

"Go away!" yelled Sasha. "I'm not opening the door!"

"Please!" said Jade.

"No," insisted Sasha. "It's too awful!"

"We've got to get in there and see what happened," said Yasmin, wondering what could be so bad that it had totally rattled their usually calm and collected friend.

"It can't be that bad!" Jade shouted.

"You haven't seen my hair!" Sasha yelled back. "It's horrifying!"

"You have to come out sometime," Cloe called through the door.

"Not in this lifetime!" Sasha shouted.

The other three girls agreed that the situation called for emergency measures. Cloe suggested going around the back of the lodge and climbing through the window, which they'd left open that morning. If they lifted each other up, they could scale the embankment.

It was worth a try.

As the three of them went outside, they talked about their friend. "So much for convincing Sasha she has good luck," moaned Jade. "This has probably reversed all our other efforts."

"Yeah, seriously," added Cloe. "Thanks to the Tweevils, now she probably thinks she's majorly *unlucky*."

As they snuck around the back of the lodge, they tried to spot the window of their room. "There it is!" shouted Jade, noticing the row of scented candles she'd set up along the ledge. The girls stood below the window and looked up, trying to figure out how they could get to it.

Even though their room was on the first floor, the embankment was higher than they'd realized. How would they get up there? The girls were stumped.

"A ladder would be good," suggested Jade.

"And we would get that . . . *where*?" asked Cloe.

Jade tried making a human stepladder by lacing her fingers together and having Cloe climb up to look in the window. As Cloe teetered on Jade's hands, they heard a voice call out, "Hey, ladies!"

Cloe turned around and saw Topher and Skye walking on a footpath nearby. "Need a hand?" asked Topher, putting down his kayak paddle. He and Skye walked over to the girls.

The girls looked at each other helplessly. They knew what they were doing looked pretty suspicious.

"This is not what it looks like," Cloe said.

"Well, that's good," Skye replied. "Because it looks like you're breaking and entering."

"Well, we are — but to our own room," Yasmin explained.

Topher turned to smile at her. "I don't believe we've met," he said, and Yasmin was dazzled by his bright green eyes and friendly smile.

"I'm Yasmin," she replied. "And I swear, I'm not a criminal."

"None of us are!" Jade chimed in.

"Okay, then what exactly is going on here?"

Topher asked. "Because if you just locked your-selves out, I'm sure the lodge can give you a replacement key."

"It's not that," Jade explained. "See, our friend Sasha used some bad hair product, and now she's locked herself in the bathroom and won't come out."

"So now we're on a rescue mission!" Cloe fin-ished.

"Well, that does sound like a good cause," Skye said.

"Though I'll never understand how a girl could get that upset over a bad hair day," Topher added.

"Hey, it's upsetting!" Jade protested. The boys just grinned at her.

"Will you lift me up?" Cloe asked.

"Happy to help," Topher replied. He and Skye set down their bags and hoisted Cloe up to the window ledge. She peered inside, but couldn't see Sasha.

"Bunny Boo!" she called.

"Cloe?" Sasha asked, sniffling. "Where are you?"

"I climbed up to the window to see if you were okay," Cloe explained. "If you won't come out, I guess I'll just have to come in!"

"No, it's too dangerous to crawl through the window," Sasha protested. "I'd never forgive myself if you got hurt trying to help me through my hair crisis."

"Does that mean you'll come out if I come back to the room?" Cloe asked.

"Okay . . ." Sasha said slowly. "But you have to promise not to laugh!"

"Of course we won't laugh!" Cloe exclaimed, wondering what exactly could have happened to her best friend's hair. "Okay, boys, bring me down!" she called. Back on the ground, she grabbed the girls and raced back toward their room before Sasha could change her mind. "Thanks guys! We'll see you tonight!" she shouted over her shoulder.

Back at the room, Sasha peeked out of the bathroom with a towel wrapped around her head. "Come in," she whispered to her three best friends.

The girls filed in, and Sasha closed the bathroom door behind them. Then, taking a deep breath, Sasha removed her towel. Her friends couldn't believe what they saw.

Chapter 10

"Your hair is green!" Cloe exclaimed in shock.

Actually, it wasn't *completely* green, but it did have some awfully big green streaks in it. Everyone stared and murmured. No one had ever seen anything quite like it before.

Sasha burst into tears. "I've tried everything," she said. "I shampooed, I rinsed, I repeated. What should I do?" For a moment, there was silence.

"Don't do anything," blurted Jade. "It's perfect just the way it is."

"What?" the girls demanded in unison, staring at Jade. Was she serious? Now Yasmin and Cloe took a second look at the dramatic green streaks and looked at each other. Jade was right.

The streaks were awesome.

Suddenly, everyone was speaking at once. "You're totally in the St. Patrick's Day spirit," said Jade admiringly. "Think how fab your hair is going to look when you throw some green accents into your outfit. It's outrageous."

"Re . . . really?" stammered Sasha, surprised by their reaction.

"Talk about making a splash! You're really going to turn heads at the party tonight," said Yasmin.

"Hey, I want green streaks in my hair too!" Cloe

exclaimed. She grabbed the hair mascara and swiped a long streak into her blonde hair.

"Lovin' it!" said Jade.

All four of them crowded in front of the bathroom mirror. They passed around the mascara and painted their hair with glittering green highlights. It was a fresh, sassy, and totally unique holiday look!

"Gorgeous!" Cloe declared, admiring herself in the mirror. When all four of them put their heads together, the effect was spectacular.

"Well, I think we all know what this calls for," said Jade.

"Shopping!" shouted Cloe, Sasha, and Yasmin at the same time.

They had a few hours before the party to rig up some out-of-this-world outfits. Only now they had to be creative: What green accessories could they come up with to play up their dazzling hairdos?

"As my bumper sticker says, 'Go Green!'" said Cloe. She and her friends were totally into saving the environment, and now she was "going green" in her wardrobe, too!

"But where can we go shopping around here?" asked Yasmin. "There's not exactly a Misty Mountain Mall."

"True, Pretty Princess," said Cloe. "But the lodge gift shop might have some pretty cool odds and ends." It would be a creative challenge to find green-accented accessories, but these girls were fashion geniuses.

The Bratz agreed to tuck their hair into their neon-colored bandannas and check out the boutique. They didn't want anyone to see their green locks before they had their chance to make a grand entrance at the party.

They looked around the gift shop and brain-stormed. A few items jumped out at them right away, like a jade pendant, a metallic green belt, and a bright plastic bangle bracelet. *That was a start*, thought Cloe, but they needed a few more accent pieces.

Walking out of the store, they clutched their plastic shopping bags and put their heads together. "How about making a run to the nearest mall?" Sasha suggested. They went over to Cloe's car to look at a map.

"Hmmm," said Cloe, looking at the map she had unfolded in the front seat. "There's a shopping center in Springville," she said, "but this map says the town is an hour away," she said. "I think that's too long a drive for this late in the day."

"And it would interfere with getting ready," said Yasmin. "I need time to take a strawberry bubble bath and put on a face mask."

The girls agreed that a long drive was out of the question. Jade looked out the window and saw the white-haired old man from the stable walking to his car. "Hey, Mr. Dooley!" she called out.

The man smiled and walked over to the girls, who were leaning against the car. "Hello, girls," he said warmly. Noticing the looks on their faces, he asked what was wrong.

"We just wish there were some stores around here," said Cloe. "There's this big party tonight at the lodge . . ."

"What is it that you need?" he asked.

"Some cool stuff to go with our outfits," said Sasha. "Belts, necklaces, hats, purses — you know, all the essentials!"

The old man thought for a moment. "Take your car and follow me down the road for a mile," he said "I think I can help you."

The Bratz looked at each other and raised their eyebrows. How sweet! But where could the old man be taking them? There weren't any stores around for miles.

Cloe followed Mr. Dooley's pickup truck down the single-lane road. When he turned into a driveway, Cloe trailed behind until they arrived at a wooden barn. A sign on the barn said Misty Mountain Theater.

Mr. Dooley got out of his truck and came over to them. "Don't know if this will help," he said. "But I volunteer here and we have a costume shop." He unlocked the door to the barn and led them inside to a big room filled with racks of colorful garments.

Wow! The Bratz were dazzled by all the eye-catching fabrics and props. There were clothes for milkmaids and pirates, queens and court jesters. "If you see something you like, I'd be happy to lend it to you for tonight, so long as you write down what you take."

The girls squealed in excitement. This was a fashionista's dream come true!

"Thank you so much, Mr. Dooley," Cloe gushed. "You've totally saved the day!"

"Happy to help," the old man said.

The girls scoured the racks for cool accessories. Among hoop skirts and armor were the most unbelievable treasures: a full dark-green skirt, a pair of lime-green ballet slippers, and some sparkly green barrettes.

After stuffing their goodies into Cloe's trunk, they thanked Mr. Dooley over and over, promising to return everything the next day. Pulling away from the theater, they waved good-bye to the white-haired man.

"You know, he kind of looks like a leprechaun," said Sasha, observing his spry figure from a distance. Cloe and Jade exchanged glances. Maybe their friend was finally getting into the holiday spirit!

Now they had their work cut out for them. As soon as they were back in the room, they took their new accessories and tried out different combinations. "This is so much fun," said Jade, trying on a pair of sequined ballet slippers.

In a flurry of hairbrushes, eye makeup, and jewelry, the girls got ready for the party. Finally, they were ready to make their big entrance.

"We look fantastic," said Cloe, looking over everyone. She wore a ruffled black miniskirt with a silver costume belt and a black top with green fringe. Silvery-green earrings dangled from her ears.

Yasmin was a knockout in a green skirt and satiny white top, with her hair tied back in a bun. Green chopsticks crisscrossed in her sleek pile of hair. Jade was dramatic in a fancy military jacket, and Sasha was totally hip in a beaded green baby-doll top.

"Well," said Jade, taking a deep breath. "Time to make our debut!"

The Bratz put on their finishing touches, and gave each other hugs. They knew their holiday look was fabulous, but would the guys agree?

Mustering all their bravery, they headed downstairs to the great room and paused a moment before opening the door.

The girls took a deep breath and clutched each other's hands.

"It's now or never," Sasha declared, and pushed open the door.

Chapter 11

As soon as the door opened, everyone in the room turned and gasped. No one had expected such dramatic looks for a little outdoor adventure club party!

Everyone stared as the girls strutted in, their green, silver, and gold accessories glittering under the lights.

Topher's jaw dropped when he saw them. Were these divas the same girls he'd seen in workout clothes just a few hours before? "You girls look gorgeous," he murmured.

Suddenly, the Bratz were mobbed. The members of the Outdoor Adventure Club tripped over each other to meet the new guests. Cloe, Sasha, Jade, and Yasmin turned to each other in relief: their new look was a hit!

Sasha looked around at the scene before her. Strands of colored lights were draped across the beamed ceiling. A fire was blazing in the big stone fireplace, and platters of burgers and corn were served fresh off the grill. A DJ was spinning an awesome dance mix.

This party rocked.

It didn't hurt that the adventure club members were warm, friendly, and *cute*! They kept coming up and offering to get the girls something to eat or drink. "Love your hair!" they kept saying.

In fact, they were having such a spectacular time that they didn't even notice the Tweevils cowering in the corner.

"I can't believe those obnoxious Bratz," complained Kirstee. "They're supposed to be mortified by their green hair, not proud of it!" Her little "gift" for Sasha had backfired in a big way.

Who knew the Bratz could turn green hair into a fashion statement?

"They've turned the whole hair-streak thing around," observed Kaycee. Looking at Kirstee's furious face, she wondered what she'd said wrong.

"You moron," said Kirstee seething. "Can't you see they're bigger fashion disasters than ever? They may think they look good, but nobody's buying it."

The Tweevils watched as the boys swarmed around the Bratz. "Yeah, the guys are all totally repelled by it," said Kaycee. "That's why they're all fighting to get those girls their next soda."

"Don't tell me you're jealous!" shrieked Kirstee. "Of those freaks? Of course green hair attracts attention. But that doesn't mean it's *good* attention."

Kaycee sipped her lemonade and took this in. If the Bratz were getting attention for having green hair, maybe she and her sister should get some, too. Watching the boys flocking around the Bratz made Kaycee feel totally lonely.

"I've got an idea," said Kaycee. Kirstee looked surprised — usually *she* was the one who came up with schemes.

"Let's turn our hair green, too!" said Kaycee. "We still have some of that dye left that we put in Sasha's hair mascara."

Kirstee considered the idea. She didn't like encouraging Kaycee to think on her own — that could be dangerous. On the other hand, it was annoying to watch these fashion freaks get all the attention.

"Then the Bratz wouldn't stand out as much," Kaycee continued. "And maybe the guys would pay attention to us."

Grudgingly, Kirstee agreed to go back to the room and give it a try. After all, if it had worked for the Bratz, it was sure to work even better for them!

The twins scurried back to their room, where they peeled off their party clothes and put on fluffy white bathrobes. They filled the sink with green dye, then dunked their heads into it, drenching their hair in the muddy green mixture. It had been Kaycee's idea to go with more concentrated dye — she figured if green was good, then more green was better!

"Well," said Kaycee, toweling off her head. "What do you think?"

Kristee looked in the mirror at the two of them. "It's great," she said slowly. "If you don't mind looking like you've been swimming in a swamp."

Kaycee frowned. Kirstee was right! Their hair hung down in hideous clumps, in a totally gross pea-green color. The consistency was disgusting. *Ugh*, she thought.

"I hope you're happy," snarled Kirstee. "Now we smell like medicine and our hair is the color of puke!"

"Okay, okay!" cried Kaycee. "So it wasn't my best idea. We can just try to rinse it off."

Two hours later, they were still trying, while the party went on without them.

When the clock struck midnight, the Bratz girls barely noticed. The party was still going strong, and they were having a blast laughing and dancing with their new friends. Suddenly, Cloe felt Sasha tugging on her arm.

"Hey Angel," she whispered. "We've got to go! We've got facials scheduled, and then we have to race home to do our essays for creative writing."

Cloe moaned. "But we're having such a good time here!" she said, licking chocolate off her fingers. For dessert, the club had set up a "Make Your Own S'more Table," with chocolate bars, graham crackers, and gooey marshmallows.

"Yeah," said Yasmin. "This party is fantastic."

Jade came over to join the pow-wow. "Sasha's right," she said. "We've got a lot to do tomorrow."

It had been a wonderful evening, Cloe thought wistfully, as she bobbed her head to the beat. She looked around for Topher and Skye, but didn't see them. She figured they must've headed to bed already. Oh well, she thought — they'd definitely run into the guys tomorrow.

The Bratz waved good-bye to the Outdoor Adventure Club, gathering one last round of admiring glances. Leaving the party, they held their heads high, knowing they'd pulled off fashion magic that night.

They couldn't wait to get back to the room to talk it over. "Can you believe how shocked everyone was when we first walked in?" asked Yasmin, as they headed upstairs in the hallway.

"And that look on Kirstee's face when she saw what a splash we made," said Sasha. "That was priceless!"

Back in their room, the girls hugged and high-fived each other.

"That was, like, the perfect night," Cloe sighed.

"If only every fashion disaster could turn out that well!" Jade added.

After they'd changed into their pajamas, they gathered on Cloe's bed for the best part of any gathering — the post-party gossip. They chattered for hours about the cute boys they'd met, until finally Sasha said, "Okay, girls, time for bed!" The others groaned, but they knew Sasha was right.

As Sasha climbed into bed, she noticed something glinting on her pillow. "What's this?" she asked, picking up the tiny golden star charm.

"I got one too!" Yasmin exclaimed, holding up an identical charm.

"Me too!" Cloe gasped.

"This is gorgeous," Jade sighed. "But if we all got one, then who got them for us?"

The girls all shrugged, too tired and happy to think about it anymore tonight. They all set their new lucky stars on their bedside table, and within five minutes of turning out the light, they were all fast asleep.

Chapter 12

The next day, the girls were happy to see their colorful streaks had faded. "Green hair made us look dramatic last night," said Jade. "But it's definitely *not* a daytime look."

Cloe nodded, enjoying her cinnamon French toast in the lodge dining room. "I'm glad we were able to squeeze in a facial this morning," she said. "I'm looking forward to chillin' at the spa."

A few minutes later, the four of them checked

into the spa and hit the locker room. When Cloe went to wash her hands, she saw Kirstee and Kaycee bent over one of the sinks.

"Try rinsing it again," ordered Kirstee.

"I told you," whined Kaycee. "It's not working!"

Cloe, Yasmin, Jade, and Sasha exchanged glances. The Tweevils' hair was a sickening shade of pea green.

Kirstee noticed the Bratz standing behind them. "What do *you* want?" she growled. "If you guys hadn't paraded around like green divas, then we wouldn't be in this mess."

"I'm sorry, I don't remember sneaking green dye into your hair products," Jade snapped.

"Nope — I'm actually pretty sure that's something *you* did to *us*," Sasha added.

"We tried to dye our hair too," Kaycee complained. "But it turned this awful color."

"That's why it's important to find your own

personal sense of style — *not* to rip off someone else's," Yasmin said.

The Bratz couldn't help but feeling a little bit glad that the Tweevils had gotten a taste of their own medicine.

After their treatments, they returned to the changing room, where the Tweevils were still scrubbing. Sasha took pity on them and pulled a plastic bottle out of her gym bag, handing it to Kaycee. "Hair color rinse," Kaycee read off the label.

"I just bought it at the spa, and we all used it on our hair," Sasha said. "As you can see, it totally works." She gestured to her friends' hair, all returned to their normal lustrous shades. "And we won't be needing it anymore — unless you have any more plans to sabotage our hairdos?"

Kaycee shook her head, looking at the bottle uncertainly. "Hey, Kirstee, should we trust them?" she asked her sister as the Bratz walked away.

"Might as well," Kirstee muttered. "It's not like our hair could look any worse." She and her sister poured the treatment over their green heads and kept scrubbing away.

In the meantime, the Bratz hurried back to their room, gathered up their things, and crammed it in the car, wondering how they always managed to end up with so much more stuff at the end of a vacation than they'd brought at the beginning. First they stopped off at the Misty Mountain Theater, and were happy to see that Mr. Dooley was straightening up the costume shop.

"This is everything," Jade told him. "It was totally perfect!"

"We really can't thank you enough!" Yasmin added.

"My pleasure," Mr. Dooley replied.

Jade hugged Mr. Dooley and gave him a St.

Patrick's Day card with a four-leaf clover on it. Inside, the Bratz had all written thank-you messages to their new friend.

"That's very sweet of you girls," Mr. Dooley said. Then he noticed their matching star charms, which they'd all put onto their charm bracelets that morning. "Those are lovely," he said. "Where did you get them?"

"Actually," Sasha said, "we aren't quite sure."

"Thanks again," Cloe called as the four girls hurried back to the car.

As Cloe drove them home, the girls resumed their recap of last night's party. Suddenly, Cloe slapped her hand against her forehead.

"Oh no!" she cried. "We never said good-bye to Topher and Skye!"

"We didn't even get their phone numbers," Sasha sighed. "Now we have no way to keep in touch with them." She couldn't believe they'd been in such a hurry that morning that they'd completely forgotten about the guys.

Cloe remembered how Topher and Skye had rescued them when their canoe tipped over. It bummed her out to think she'd probably never see them again. "At least I got some cute pictures of them," she said sadly.

A few minutes later, the girls pulled into a rest stop. After buying bottles of water for everyone, Sasha waited for her friends outside. She felt a tap on her shoulder. "Did you forget something?" a boy's voice asked.

She turned to see Topher holding up a wishbone pendant. "Topher!" she cried happily.

"I spotted this in the parking lot and knew you guys were nearby," he said. "I'm really glad we found you." Skye ran up and gave her a hug.

When the Bratz emerged from the store, they greeted the boys excitedly. Topher invited them to join the outdoor club for an upcoming ski weekend, and the Bratz accepted right away. As they waved good-bye to them, the girls marveled over their good luck in running into them at the rest stop.

"Now we've got their numbers — *and* an invitation to go skiing," said Yasmin. "If that's not good luck, I don't know what is!"

Sasha considered this. "You know," she said. "I still don't believe in luck."

Cloe, Yasmin, and Jade exchanged exasperated looks. After all of their efforts, Sasha *still* didn't believe in luck?

"But I *do* believe in my friends," said Sasha. "And the three of you are the *best* good-luck charms a girl could have," she said, throwing her arms around the other girls. "You cheered me up when I was totally down about writing the essay. You got me to come on this trip, which I'm *so* glad I didn't miss, and you surprised me with lots of presents to make me feel special," she explained. "What could be luckier than that?"

The other girls thought about that for a moment. "You're right," said Cloe. "We are each others' good-luck charms. We help each other and show each other the bright side of things," she said thoughtfully. "That's what you should write about in your essay!"

Sasha looked at Cloe gratefully. "Thanks, Angel. I guess I have more to say about being lucky than I realized." Suddenly, she couldn't wait to start the assignment.

"Hey, I wish I'd thought of that myself," chimed in Jade. "That's more interesting than writing about my lucky notebook."

From the driver's seat, Cloe looked over at Sasha again. "So you knew the wishbone pendant and the horseshoe and the bamboo were from us?" she said. Sasha nodded. "But how about the charms we found on our pillows last night?" asked Cloe.

Sasha looked surprised. "I thought one of you guys had given those to everyone to throw me off the trail," she said. The girls looked at each other. They had just assumed the charms were a present from Sasha, since she'd figured out they were giving her all those gifts.

If it wasn't her, who was it?

Each of the girls looked down at the new charms dangling from their bracelets. "Are you thinking what I'm thinking?" asked Yasmin.

"Maybe there really was some luck in the air this weekend," said Cloe excitedly. "How cool is that?"

The girls smiled happily. Pretty cool, indeed.